Firefighter

Lucy M. George

Ando Twin

Frank is a firefighter.
It's a very busy job!

When he arrives at work, he puts on his special clothes and tests all the equipment.

"It's time for the fire drill!" Frank calls to his crew.

Everyone has a special job, so when there's an emergency they can work together quickly.

The alarm bell rings!

RRRIIINNNGGG!!!!

"There's a fire at the school!" calls the watch manager.

Frank slides down the pole...

"GO!" he shouts.

At the school, there are bright flames
and smoke coming from the window!

The children are lined up safely in the playground.
The teachers are taking the register
to make sure no one is inside.

Mr Jones, the head teacher, points up at the window.

"The fire is in the library. Everyone is safe except Gerald the guinea pig. Please save him if you can!" he says.

Frank and his crew must get up to the library quickly!

The crew put on their masks to protect them from breathing in smoke.

Some of the crew fix the hoses to a fire hydrant and the others go into the school through the main door.

Frank climbs onto the turntable ladder on the back of the fire engine. It lifts him up high.

Frank looks through the window to check that it is safe to enter.

Then he carefully climbs inside.

There is lots of smoke in the library. The flames are bright red and very hot!

The rest of the crew rush
upstairs to help Frank.

The children
watch from
the playground.

Finally, Frank comes to
the window and calls
down, "The fire is out...
and Gerald is okay!"

"Hooray!" the
children cheer.

An ambulance arrives to make sure that no one
is hurt. The paramedics check the children
and teachers, but everyone is fine.

The crew
make sure the school is
safe. They open windows
to help the smoke clear. Then
they put all their kit away.

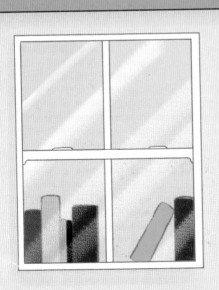

Frank is very happy because everyone did
the right thing during the fire and no one
was hurt... not even Gerald the guinea pig!

What else does Frank do?

Teaches people about fire safety.

Checks fire hydrants are working.

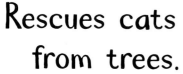
Rescues cats from trees.

Helps people in road accidents.

Keeps fit and strong.

What does Frank need?

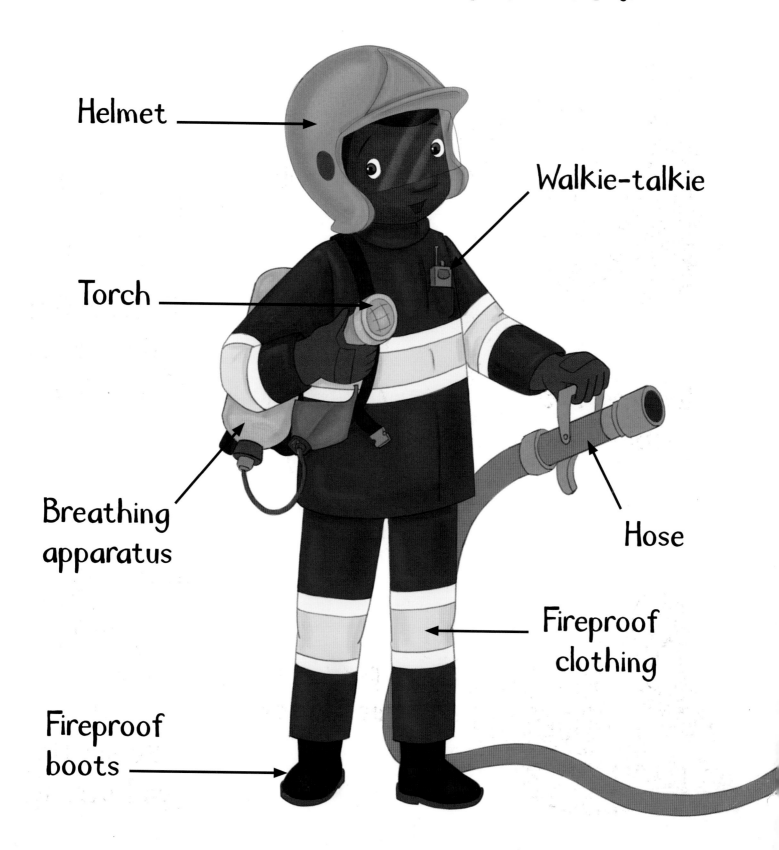

Helmet

Walkie-talkie

Torch

Breathing apparatus

Hose

Fireproof clothing

Fireproof boots

Other busy people

Here are some of the other busy people firefighters work with.

Paramedics help people at an accident and take them to hospital if they are hurt. They carry medical kits and are specially trained to help people in an emergency.

Police officers sometimes come to a fire to help keep everything in order.

Call handlers answer 999 calls. They decide what kind of help is needed and sometimes stay on the phone until the emergency services arrive. They are trained to stay calm and speak clearly.

Watch managers send firefighters out to help people when emergency calls come in.

Next steps

- Discuss the dangers of fire and why we should never play with it.

- What could cause a fire at home or at school? Help the children think of what they can do to help prevent a fire.

- Have the children ever had a fire drill at school? Go over what the children should do during a fire drill. Why should they always tell a teacher or grown up where they are going?

- Has a smoke alarm ever gone off at home? What happened? Ask the children to find the smoke alarms in their homes.

- Ask the children if they have ever been in a fire engine, or to a fire station. Do they know any firefighters?

- Talk about the other busy people firefighters work with. Discuss the different jobs and what they might involve. Which job would the children most like to do?

Quarto is the authority on a wide range of topics.

Quarto educates, entertains and enriches the lives of our readers—enthusiasts and lovers of hands-on living.

www.quartoknows.com

Publisher: Zeta Jones
Associate Publisher: Maxime Boucknooghe
Editorial Director: Victoria Garrard
Art Director: Laura Roberts-Jensen
Editor: Sophie Hallam
Designer: Anna Lubecka

Copyright © QED Publishing 2015

First published in the UK in 2015 by
QED Publishing
Part of The Quarto Group,
The Old Brewery, 6 Blundell Street, London, N7 9BH

www.quartoknows.com/brand/2040/QED-Publishing/

A catalogue record for this book is available from the British Library.

ISBN 978 1 78493 151 3

Printed in China

**For Granny Wilson
- AndoTwin**

**For Rose & Alex
- Lucy M. George**